CROSS
CROCODILE

First published in 2009 by Hodder Children's Books
This paperback edition published in 2010

Text copyright © Bruce Hobson 2009
Illustrations copyright © Adrienne Kennaway 2009
www.brucehobson.net

Hodder Children's Books, 338 Euston Road, London, NW1 3BH

Hodder Children's Books Australia
Level 17/207 Kent Street, Sydney, NSW 2000

A catalogue record of this book is available from the British Library.

ISBN: 978 0 340 97033 1

Printed in China.

Hodder Children's Books is a division of Hachette Children's Books.
An Hachette UK Company.
www.hachette.co.uk

CROSS CROCODILE

Written by
Mwenye Hadithi

Illustrated by
Adrienne Kennaway

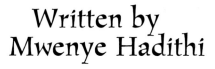

Hodder
Children's
Books

A division of Hachette Children's Books

Long ago on the Great African Plains, it was so dry before the rain came that all the grass was brown and tough, and all the animals were hot, and thirsty, and hungry.

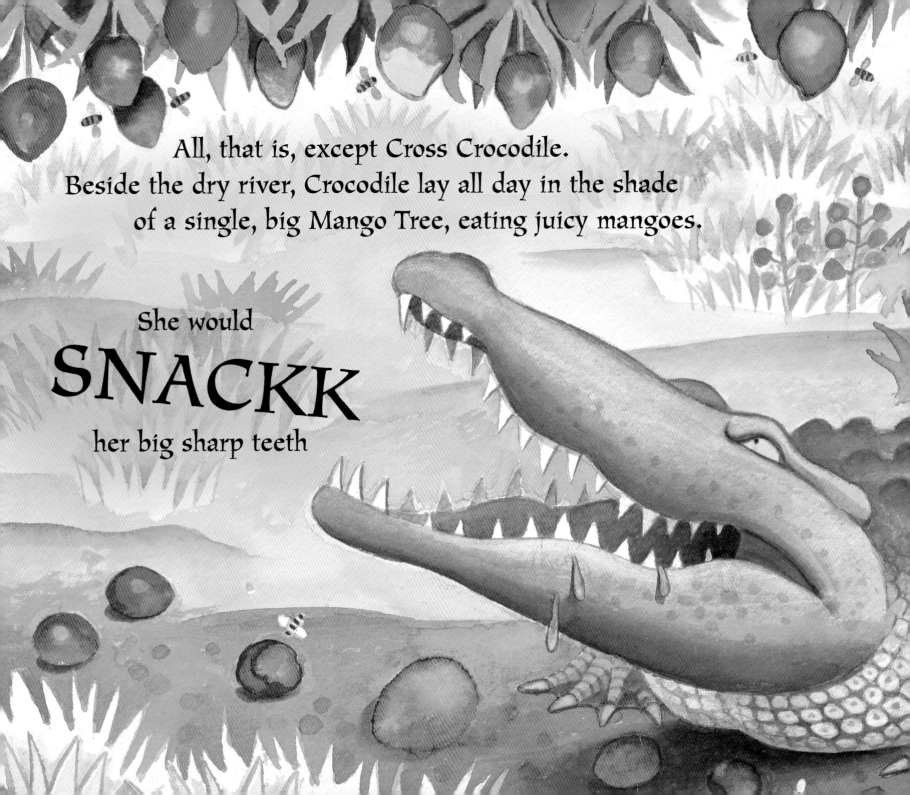

All, that is, except Cross Crocodile.
Beside the dry river, Crocodile lay all day in the shade
of a single, big Mango Tree, eating juicy mangoes.

She would

SNACKK

her big sharp teeth

and *SWISSH*
her huge tail at anyone who came close.

"We are so hungry and thirsty, what shall we do?"
cried the animals. "Crocodile is so cross and mean,
she won't even share one mango!"

Monkey sat on the dusty plain
listening to the wind, and suddenly
thought of a plan...

Next morning all the animals gathered at the edge of the forest where Monkey was rolling hollow logs until they were all in a line, leading towards the Mango Tree.

"Elephant, Hyena, the Wild Dogs, and all animals with loud voices must wait by these hollow logs," said Monkey.

"When you see me raise my arms above my head then you must all howl down the hollow logs!"

"Now, Eagle, Bush Baby, Squirrel, and all the animals who live in the trees, must go and sit quietly up in the tree-tops by the Mango Tree," said Monkey.

"When you see me scratch my head with both hands then you must all flap about and jump up and down!"

Then Monkey ran off over the hill
to visit the Weaver Birds.

When Monkey came back to
Crocodile he was carrying a large, thick
rope of vines made by the Weaver Birds.

"Quick!" called Monkey. "You must run!
A big wind is coming that will blow all
the animals off the earth!"

"Nothing can
blow me off the
earth," snorted
Crocodile crossly.

Then Monkey scratched his head with both hands.

Eagle, Bush Baby, Squirrel, and all the animals who lived in the trees, flapped their wings and jumped up and down, causing the leaves to shake and the trees to tremble.

"What is that?" cried Crocodile.

"I told you, it is the big wind!" said Monkey. "I must tie down the other animals or they will be blown off the earth!"

"Nothing can blow me away,"
said Crocodile rather nervously.

Then Monkey raised his arms
above his head.

Elephant, Hyena, the Wild Dogs,
and all animals with loud voices
howled down the hollow logs.

Now Cross Crocodile was feeling scared.
"What can I do? Help me! I cannot run very fast like you!"

Monkey raised his arms above his head, and then he
also scratched his head with both hands.

And all the trees on the plain
shook with the
sound of a howling wind.

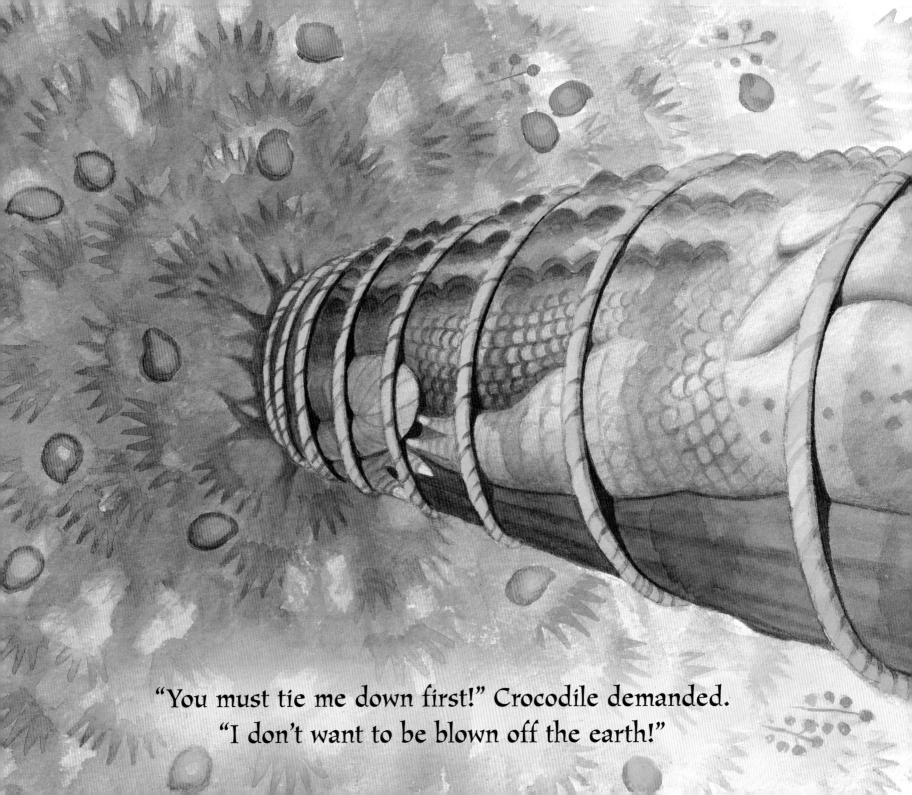

"You must tie me down first!" Crocodile demanded.
"I don't want to be blown off the earth!"

"Very well," agreed Monkey.
"I will tie you to the tree. Hurry!"

So Monkey tied Crocodile to the tree,
tight as tight as tight.

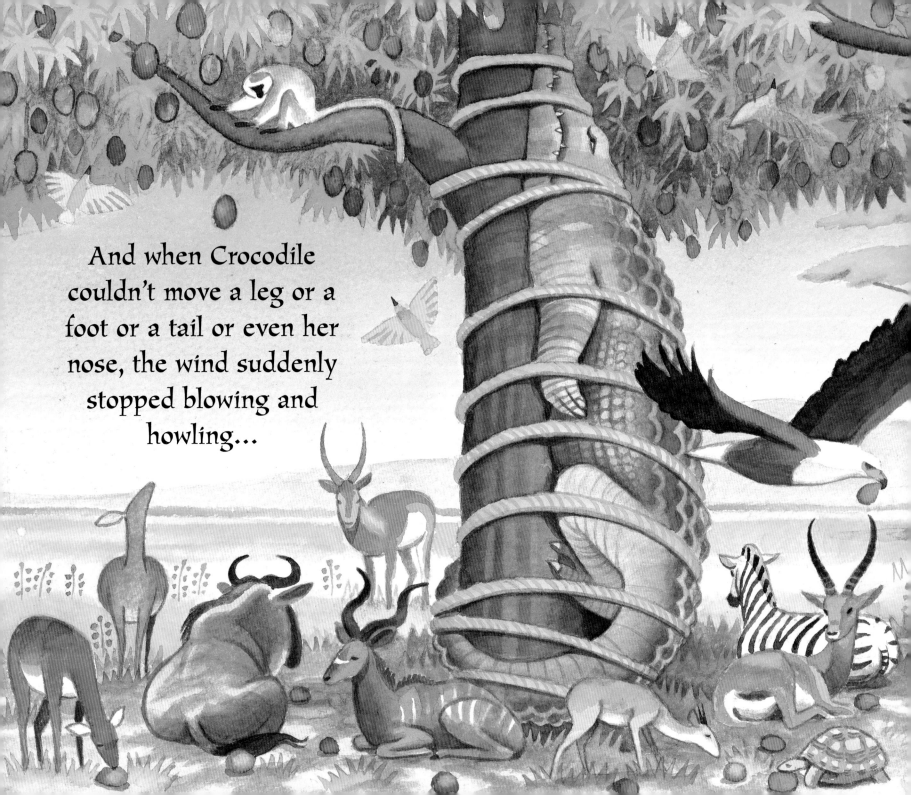

And when Crocodile couldn't move a leg or a foot or a tail or even her nose, the wind suddenly stopped blowing and howling...

...and all the animals came and sat in the shade of the big Mango Tree and ate juicy mango fruit until they were full.

Cross Crocodile
wriggled all evening,
and wriggled
all night.

As the sun came up Crocodile finally broke free. As soon as she saw Monkey she began to chase him and chase him, round and up and round and down, but she couldn't catch him.

And even today Crocodile
hides just below the surface
in the river, waiting with just
her eyes and the end of her
nose showing.

She doesn't move because she
is still hoping that maybe,
just maybe, today will
be the day that she finally
catches Monkey.